BEAUTIFUL SOLITUDE

The real world—it had broken her. The shame of being overwhelmed by it all crushed her, like the crunching of leaves beneath her feet as she walked the overgrown footpath. She thought a trip away, alone, would reduce the stress that sat like a giant on her chest. Yet, the atmosphere was drab. The silence was maddening. And she was certain she was lost.

How is someone supposed to stay on track around here if every group of trees looks the same?

The emails piling up in her inbox and voicemails being left at a rapid speed consumed her thoughts. Tess's gaze was unfocused as she plodded along, looking at the forest, yet seeing only unfinished tasks and daunting deadlines.

I shouldn't be thinking of that. I should focus on the trail.

A single cabin dropped in the middle of one hundred acres—she could not have asked for more seclusion if she tried. The Airbnb listing stated that it only took a quick, three-mile hike to reach the center of beautiful solitude.

A gale blew through the trees, whistling as it whipped her hair around her ears. The gusts that trilled and snaked through the branches carried notes that sounded nearly human; the sound sent chills down her spine. When a twig snapped behind her, she pivoted in a flash. Shallow breaths left her lips, and the wind died down, leaving only her quick inhales and exhales.

The scene before her was the same as all the others: looming oaks, a sloping valley, and a poor excuse for a trail. Nothing moved, and not a single sound met her ears other than the drumming of her panicked heart. After another moment of cautious silence, she turned and stalked down the trail with purpose. *I just want to find this damn cabin.*

Snap!

Another twig cracked behind her, and she swung around once more. Still nothing. Aggravation built in her veins.

Beautiful solitude? More like a creepy, dilapidated forest that only a psychopath could enjoy.

Her mother had told her not to jump headfirst into this job. Her whole purpose is fixing others' mistakes—to be

What Comes Before

Before

Molly Macabre

CONTENTS

To my husband,

who has always been my calm in the storm.

at the beck and call of the richest scumbags the world had spat out, except maybe her father. Their constant crying when they faced the consequences of their actions made her stomach churn. After a day of keeping her feelings bottled up, and resisting the urge to tell them they had gotten what they deserved, she would often feel physically ill.

Her mother warned her that it would consume her life and destroy her well-being.

Here I am again...playing the part of the spiteful daughter.

She jogged down the trail now, which was upsetting because she was not in shape at all. Her heart hammered between the fear and the forced exercise.

Crack!

This one sounded louder, a small branch, and when she spun around, she lost her footing against the side of the trail. Her ankle twisted, and she slipped on a pile of moist leaves. Her hands flailed, desperate to grasp onto anything. When they came up short, her body shuffled down the hill until she tripped over a stump. Her shin scraped against the rough wood, and she lost her balance.

Tess's body was rolling now. She reached for dirt and leaves, only succeeded at pulling sediment down into the valley with her. Her backpack snagged on a rock, jerking her body violently. Tess hoped the interference would be enough to slow her tumble. Instead, the rock broke free of the soil, and she continued downward.

The tumble picked up speed until she was a clumsy tangle of limbs barrelling along the ground. Almost at the bottom, her head cracked against something solid. Pain ignited in her temples, and her vision blurred. A mist covered the ground of the ravine, and when she looked around, there was something several feet away. A shadow of a person, except it had no features. No face.

Tess blinked repeatedly, trying to banish the fog over-taking her consciousness. Her efforts were futile, and the world went dark.

2

THE QUEST FOR RESPITE

"Hey, are you okay?" The voice was muffled as it reached her ears. Tess blinked away the blurry swirls of gray that swam in her vision. A trickle of warm liquid slid down her forehead. A hand jutted out to grab her forearm when she tried to sit up. "Woah, take it easy. You hit your head."

Tess's vision cleared, and she was face to face with a man sitting on the ground beside her wearing gray khaki hiking pants and an army green button-up shirt. Rogue strands of oily blonde hair sprouted in various directions on his head, some matted to his skin from sweat. His face was gentle as he regarded her with a look of concern.

"Who are you?" Tess sat up slowly. Aches skittered across her body as she repositioned herself.

"Aiden," he answered in a somewhat melancholic tone.

"I'm Tess, I think," she winced as a jolt of pain seared through her skull.

"Probably, you look like a Tess." Aiden pulled his arms out of the backpack straps and unzipped his bag. He took out a first aid kit, where he retrieved gauze and alcohol. "Can I?" Aiden gestured to Tess's head. Without thinking, her fingers grazed the gash at her hairline.

"Yeah, sure."

Aiden delicately cleaned blood and debris from the open cut splitting the skin at the top of her forehead, then placed a bandage across it.

"Where did you come from?" Tess asked. Aiden glanced around the woods as if he were just noticing his surroundings.

"I used to camp here all the time as a kid. Thought I'd come out and do some hiking today, for nostalgia's sake."

"And how's that going for you?" Tess stood on shaky legs.

"I think I'm a bit turned around."

Tess nodded. "There's a trail just up the hill. I've been following it to get to the cabin. I just...haven't come across it yet."

"Let's head up and see what we can find."

Tess and Aiden started up the hill. The strain of the incline burned her calves. A wind rushed through the trees, blowing leaves around in a spiral. A strangled moan floated in the air, making Tess pause.

"Did you hear that?" she asked. Aiden did not meet her gaze.

"Hear what?"

"Never mind." Tess and Aiden reached the top of the ravine, out of breath.

"What the hell?" Tess gasped. She looked from left to right frantically. Aiden raised his eyebrows and looked around.

"What's wrong?" Aiden asked.

Tess pointed at the ground, her mouth agape. "The trail. There *was* a trail here. Unless...but I fell downward, not sideways!"

"The trail wasn't a great one anyway. We probably just came up to the part where it gets lost in the woods," Aiden's tone was comforting, though Tess was unsettled by how calm he was.

Cold air prickled at Tess's skin, causing goosebumps to erupt across her flesh. She pulled her bookbag around and retrieved a sweatshirt. The navy blue letters stood out against the heather gray fabric. *Viremont University*. Tess's mother had bought it for her from the university store on her first day, gazing at her new freshman with weary, sagging eyes full of love. Tess wrapped herself in the sweatshirt, wishing it were a warm hug from the woman who provided her with unconditional support.

"Ready to keep going?" Aiden asked.

Tess was not ready. She figured if she headed back now, she could reach her car before night fell. Then what? Tess would get in her car, head back to town, open those damned emails and get back to the job that was ripping her apart. With clenched fists, Tess nodded to Aiden. Determination flooded her, and she would not give up easily.

Tess and Aiden walked atop the hill in the direction of the supposed cabin. After an hour had passed, Tess started to doubt their destination existed at all.

"Have you ever been to the cabin?" Tess asked.

"Yeah, I used to come across it from time to time. It's been a while since I've been out here, though."

A crackle of thunder, or what Tess believed was thunder, roared through the air. The rumble echoed steadily. Rather than emitting from the sky, it swam through the trees. The sound grew until Tess was certain that whatever was causing the sound was approaching them.

Aiden came to a standstill, eyes wide and glancing around carefully.

"What is that?" Tess asked, and Aiden promptly shushed her.

The clamor ripped through the trees until it was upon them.

"Get down!" Aiden shrieked and pulled Tess down against the base of a tree. All around them, branches cracked in half and leaves pelted the ground. The sound grew to a furious howl, as though a pained giant was ripping apart the forest around them.

Smaller trees capsized into the dirt. Branches whipped against Tess's body, and she screamed. Aiden pulled her tighter into the tree. Another branch stabbed into her arm. Blood trickled from the wound and spattered her face in the fierce wind. Aiden slung his backpack around, pulled a flare from within it, and ignited the stick. Orange light illuminated the world around them. Aiden let out a raspy shout and flung the flare.

The ominous entity seemed to flinch away from the light. The thunder moved on, bellowing through the woods away from them. As the wind ebbed, a faint sound hung just beneath the gusts. Whistling, Tess thought at first, yet it met her ears in a disjointed, staccato. When Tess fought to catch the sound, she could just make out the trills of a young girl's laughter, bouncing away from them as if skipping through a playground. Tess held her arm in pain, crying and shaking with fear.

"What the hell was that?" Tess sobbed. Aiden had already presented his first aid kit, pushing up the sleeves of her sweatshirt, now ripped to shreds, and patched her forearm.

"I don't know." His voice was a tight whisper.

"How did you know the flare would work?"

"I didn't. I wasn't sure what else to do."

Tess trembled as Aiden finished tending her wounds, terror running rampant through her as she tried to make sense of what had taken place.

"I have to get back to my car," Tess said as Aiden finished wrapping her injuries. "If we just walk the other way, back towards the trail..." The skeptical look on Aiden's face cut her short.

"Sure, we can head that way," Aiden said, packing up the supplies.

Tess stood on quavering legs, glancing around the forest as though she would see the gale that had attacked her. The atmosphere was empty, only a dreaded silence pounded against her ears as she strained to hear.

The pair walked in the direction where Tess understood the trail to be. The silence between them was filled with tension and fear. Before, giving up on her quest for respite was not an option. Now, Tess wanted to get away from this horrific place.

Twenty minutes went by, and Tess was certain the trail should have reappeared. The edge of the ravine remained alongside them to their left. In fact, she swore she saw a path of upset leaves winding down the hill—the place she had fallen. Yet there was not the slightest hint of a dirt trail.

Still, she pressed on, deducing that the path may have worn down to nothing long before she fell, and she had only been following what she assumed would lead to the cabin.

"*Tess!*"

The word sliced through the steady cadence of their hike. Tess's heart pounded beneath her chest at the familiarity of the voice—a man she had hoped to spend the weekend escaping.

"*Damnit, Tess!*"

Tess's eyes darted to Aiden. "Who is that?"

Aiden's brows scrunched. "What do you mean?"

"What do I mean? Someone just—"

"*Tess! I need those reports! Have you even contacted the newspapers yet? Get me on the phone with that lawyer! Tess! Damnit, Tess!*"

Tess closed her hands around her ears, though it did not stop the steady barrage of demands from Jacob, her boss.

"Tess, are you okay?" Aiden's voice came through muffled. Tess turned away from him and squeezed her eyes shut. The onslaught of requests in her boss's voice pummeled into her until it sounded as if he were screaming into her ears. She fell to her knees, and just as Jacob's voice reached a climax, the forest fell silent again.

Tess wheezed as tears streaked her cheeks. Aiden knelt beside her, both hands on her shoulders, repeating words of consolation. Jacob's voice echoed in her head, a violent reminder of the reason she had escaped to the woods in the first place.

After several deep breaths, Tess faced Aiden. "I'm okay."

"What happened?"

"You really didn't hear anything?" Tess wondered.

Aiden shook his head. Tess noted the way his gaze was concerned without being incredulous.

"Let's just keep walking."

3

SHOOT THE MESSENGER

The trail never reappeared. Tess and Aiden had walked for what felt like an hour without a change in scenery.

"We should stop for a break," Aiden said. He sat on the ground beside a grand maple with fiery leaves. Tess sat beside him and groped in her pack for her bottle of water. The two hydrated and shared a granola bar Tess had packed for what was supposed to be a short hike. Fear lurched in her stomach at the thought of eating their only sustenance.

"You don't happen to have a map, do you?" Tess asked.

Aiden shook his head. "No, I wish I did. I'd be long gone."

Tess pulled her cell phone from her pack. Just the sight of it sent ripples of anxiety through her. The small, black electronic was just the messenger, but there were days she would love nothing more than to shoot it. The moment she turned it on, her notifications would run wild with missed calls, voicemails, text messages, and emails.

"Doubt you'll get any service out here, but you can try," Aiden remarked.

Tess sighed, not needing much convincing to put the phone away.

"I was following a trail. The instructions for the cabin said to follow the trail, and it would lead straight to the cabin," Tess explained.

"That's the thing about this place. Everything looks alike, and it's so easy to get turned around," Aiden said.

"And apparently easy to get attacked by *nothing* and hear voices."

"You heard voices?"

"Never mind. I just want to get out of here. What if we're still here by nightfall?" The thought made her feel nauseous.

"Let's not get caught up in 'what ifs'. Let's just keep moving." Aiden stood and helped Tess to her feet. When his gaze lingered on her arms, Tess looked down to find that she had bled through her bandages. "We'll get those rewrapped when we find your car, or at least a more permanent place to rest."

Tess was thrilled when their trek took them around a bend, away from the steep trench. The view was heavily populated with maples and oaks, yet the ground had leveled. Hope bloomed in her heart.

Tess felt the weight of her pack shift just before something hit the ground with a thud and a splash. Looking around, she spotted her water bottle had fallen from her pack into a puddle of stagnant water. The spout was open and water spilled from the end of it, rippling out into the small pool. Tess knelt in the dirt and picked up the steel water bottle, closing the top tight. Aiden plodded on ahead of her as she examined the bottle and assessed how much water she had lost.

When she glanced down into the cloudy water, tired eyes and sallow cheeks stared back at her. Strands of auburn hair fell around her face in an oily mess, coated with sweat from the day's exertion. Tess's eyes burned, dry and hazy with weariness. She closed them for just a moment, wishing she were fast asleep in her queen-sized bed, buried in her goose down duvet. When Tess opened her eyes, she returned her attention to the puddle—her tiresome reflection and beatdown visage—and saw it blink. Just as she had, except moments later.

Startled, Tess stumbled backward. When she looked up, Aiden was nowhere to be seen.

"Aiden?!" Tess's words came out panicked as she looked ahead and saw only trees.

"I'm right here. You okay?" Aiden said, except from behind her. He must have backtracked while she was recovering her water.

Tess glanced back into the puddle, shutting her eyes and opening them again. This time, the reflection reacted in sync with her.

4

MIRAGE

Dusk fell over the forest like a blanket. Not the comforting, cozy kind. Tess's limbs ached, and any hope of making it back to her car had vanished. Aiden appeared tenacious, his strides just as fervent as before, though Tess noted a weariness starting to show.

Up ahead, a clearing opened up. The area within seemed two shades darker than their current environment. Something large and dim contrasted against the deep greens of the forest. Something with a linear outline. A building.

"There it is!" Tess shouted, pointing into the clearing.

"What? I don't see anything," Aiden said as he squinted his eyes toward the opening. Tess ran toward the building despite the complaints of her sore muscles.

Tess sped around a smatter of trees and stopped short just before the clearing. An elm broke her line of vision to the building, and when she came around the other side of it, she paused, staring into the area bereft of flora, mouth agape. Aiden jogged up beside her and looked between Tess and the opening.

"What is it?" he panted. Tess shook her head and felt tears forming in her eyes.

"There was... I swore I saw the cabin," Tess choked, ripping through her pack until she felt the cell phone in her hands. She held down the power button and watched the white Apple logo illuminate the screen.

"What are you doing?" Aiden asked.

"We can't just stay the night out here. We're lost, and we need help," Tess answered, her eyes glued to the phone screen.

Finally, her wallpaper appeared: a photo of Tess and her mother at dinner last year on Mother's Day. Her phone searched for service for several minutes with no success.

"I don't think you'll be able to reach anyone," Aiden said quietly.

Tess dialed the numbers anyway and stared at the phone. *Call failed.*

"Ugh," Tess groaned and retried the call, which failed again. Frustration boiled in her, and she hurled the phone at the closest tree. It shattered and fell to the ground.

"I'm sorry," Aiden whispered.

Shame washed over Tess for her outburst. Though Aiden was a stranger, he had been as helpful as he could be for someone else lost in this hellhole. She dropped to her knees and held her head in her hands.

"No, I'm sorry. I just...it was there. I swear, I saw a cabin!"

Aiden knelt beside her, his running shoes crunching on a pile of leaves.

"Hey, it's okay. Look, let's just hunker down for the evening. I'll start a fire. We can rest up and be fresh for the morning."

"Hunker down where?" Tess asked, gazing around at the thick, inhospitable forest. As her eyes scanned the towering trees and dense brush, a realization hit her. During her time in these woods, Tess failed to recall a single animal sound.

Aiden stood and peered around various sections of the trees surrounding them. "The trees are pretty thick there. We'll have decent cover from any weather."

Tess nodded and followed Aiden into the shadowy thicket.

While Aiden collected larger branches, cradling them in his arms until depositing them on the ground, Tess plucked smaller sticks and twigs from the ground. Tess had never built a campfire in the woods, or anything in the woods, and was happy to follow Aiden's lead. Camping must have been one of those recreational adventures enjoyed by unbroken families, Tess assumed.

The pair collected rocks of all shapes and sizes—jagged, cracked, smooth, and gray. After clearing the ground of leaves, they arranged the rocks in a circle.

With a lighter from his pack, Aiden lit the small pyre. The flames engulfed the tinder until they were steady. Aiden added small branches on top, fueling the flames into a rolling fire.

Tess sat cross-legged on the ground. Aches inflamed her calves, and the soles of her feet felt as though she had spent the day walking across nails. Sweat-dampened fabric clung to her skin. Though she was clammy from excessive walking, the heat from the fire comforted her. The sun had set, and the forest fell prey to the night.

After getting lost in the flames, Tess glanced around for Aiden who had been collecting things from the area around them. When she spotted him, he had a bundle of leaves in his hands. He sat them beside her and piled them into a circle.

"See? Almost as nice as a real pillow," he said.

Tess laughed. The thought was generous. The idea of using a pile of leaves as a pillow made her want to cry.

"So we just sleep on the ground, then?" Tess asked.

"Got any better ideas?"

Tess shook her head.

"What brought you out here, anyway? No offense, you seem a bit out of your element." Aiden stoked the fire with a sturdy branch he had deemed the fire poker.

Tess let out a strained chuckle. "No offense taken. I am *really* out of my element. I work a stressful job that sucks the life out of me. About a week ago, I decided I needed to get away. Far away. I Googled 'remote cabins where no one can find me' and found this place... I'm kidding. A coworker had been bragging about her awesome, relaxing trip at an Airbnb so after much scrolling, I came across the cabin and booked it. I just wanted some time away from it all."

"What do you do for work?"

"I'm a public relations manager for Cypress Pharmaceuticals. It's fine. It's good money. It can just be...overwhelming at times. But who's job isn't?"

"I don't know. Some people seem to love their jobs."

"Here's to becoming one of those people someday." Tess raised her hand, fingers curled around an imaginary drink and offered a mock toast to the air. Instantly, Tess craved to feel the chilled glass in her hand, filled to the brim with Sancere. Though only in her mind, Tess escaped to her twelfth floor apartment. She melted into the cream, leather couch and stared out of the vast picture window. City lights and starry skies twinkled and danced until becoming a blur as Tess sipped the crisp white wine.

A pop from the fire broke Tess away from her reverie, and she gazed into the orange light. Night had cloaked the woods wholly, swallowing everything in its wake. With the only light being the fire's illumination, Tess felt like a performer onstage beneath a spotlight, unable to see into the veil of darkness, but the darkness had all eyes on her.

"What about you?" Tess asked.

Aiden looked up from the fire, confusion passing across his face.

"Work?" Tess clarified.

"Oh, yeah. Well, I was a firefighter for the town nearby. I don't know how familiar you are with the area, but Sacred Valley is about twenty miles from here."

"What do you do now?" Tess wondered.

"What do you mean?"

"You said you *were* a firefighter. What do you do now?"

"Oh, I was just going through some stuff. I had to take some time off," Aiden answered, casting his gaze down at the fire. Tess watched him put up his wall, brick by brick, and nodded.

Though curious to know what hardships would prevent him from working, Tess thought it best not to press the issue. Everyone she knew was fighting some sort of battle. Some days, the struggles were mere background music to life. Other days, they were suffocating. No matter the day, each person soldiered on as though nothing were wrong, because that is what life demands of people.

"Does your family still come out here on trips?" Tess opted to brighten the mood; the way Aiden's jaw tightened at the question told her she had only darkened it.

"My family...isn't around anymore."

"Oh, I'm sorry," Tess said.

"Yeah," Aiden whispered.

Aiden stoked the fire with his poker, pushing around burning logs until the flames leapt from the pit with fervor. Warmth coiled around Tess, and she yawned, eyes sagging with exhaustion. The makeshift pillow seemed appealing at this point, so she lay her head on the orange and yellow leaves.

"You should get some rest," Tess said.

"I will," Aiden responded, though he remained sitting with his arms around his knees and gaze lost to the flames.

Tess's eyes fluttered shut, and sleep found her almost immediately.

5

THE FOREST HAS TEETH

"WAKE UP!"

Tess jolted upward. The words were screamed into her left ear, which now throbbed from the deafening disturbance. Her eyes stretched wide as she searched the darkness for the source of the shout. Blackness encompassed her vision along with the haze of sleep. She panted in fear.

"Aiden?" Tess's voice trembled. She scooted backwards on her hands, fleeing something she could not see.

Leaves stirred nearby. "Tess?" Aiden's sleepy voice called out. He sounded miles away.

"Aiden, where are you?" Tess whimpered and stood up. Her hands splayed out behind her, she backed up until she hit something. A yelp escaped her, and fear crept up her throat. When she pulled her hands away, they slid against rough bark.

Just a tree. Calm down. Tess willed her body to relax, fighting through the disorientation. Her pupils started adjusting to the darkness, and a form came into view. She stumbled over a sapling attempting to escape.

"Tess, it's me," Aiden said, much closer. The form became Aiden's body, his face scrunched in concern. "What are you doing over here?"

Tess jumped when a hand touched her shoulder, though she should have been expecting Aiden to reach out for her.

"What do you mean? Where am I? I just woke up," Tess explained.

Aiden linked his arm with hers and helped her stand steady. "Tess, you're like fifty yards away from the campfire we made."

"What...I..."

"It's okay, let's get you back." Aiden guided Tess through the veiled woods until the fire pit, with its minuscule embers, appeared. Tess expected to find evidence of being dragged or some kind of scuffle. The area was just as she had left it, the spot where she had fallen asleep was untouched.

Tears formed in her eyes. Confusion and distress crashed over her in tangible waves, nearly knocking her to the ground.

"There's something seriously wrong with this place!" Tess shouted.

"Shh, please don't be so loud," Aiden pleaded.

"Oh, we're gonna wake someone up? Please," Tess scoffed.

"Whatever attacked you earlier. I just don't want to draw attention to us."

"We don't even know what that was…"

Tess was at her wits' end. Nothing made sense.

"It's attacked me before. I did something loud. At night," Aiden said softly, his tone filled with regret.

"What happened?"

"I won't get into it now. We need to be quiet. We can talk more about it tomorrow." Aiden helped Tess to the ground and sat beside her.

"There's no way I can sleep again after this." Weariness tugged at her eyes, yet adrenaline pumped through her veins; she felt electric with fear.

"Then we'll sit here until the sun comes up."

The remainder of the night was uneventful. The pair sat side by side, waiting and watching. The forest maintained its eerie silence, making Tess feel as though the whole world were a movie on pause. The quiet pricked at her ears until she was certain the wind was moaning and the ground was shaking. She longed to converse with Aiden to distract her mind, to disrupt the lack of sound.

When the first sun rays lit up the trees, Tess felt as though she could finally breathe. Aiden's appearance did little to hide the fact that he barely slept.

"Thank goodness," Tess groaned. "I thought the sun was never going to come up."

Aiden laughed. "Same. I have a good feeling about that cabin today. Ready to move?"

"Aiden, I'm hungry," Tess implored.

"I know. Me too. We just have to keep going."

As the pair began their trek into the unknown, Tess's legs protested against each movement. Repetitive sights, her shoes on the hard ground, step after step, Tess was tired of it all. She decided that if she ever made it out, she would never hike again. This one would last her a lifetime.

A quaint trickling of water reached Tess's ears, and she looked eagerly at Aiden.

"Please, tell me you hear that," she said.

"I do! That's a good sign." Aiden's pace quickened, and Tess hurried to stay in step with him. The woods crested over a hill, and once at the top, they spotted a stream trailing through the forest on the other side.

Tess gasped. "Water! Do you think we can drink it?"

"Not unless we get desperate. It could make us sick, full of parasites and bacteria. But this creek runs to the back of the cabin. It means we're close!"

Tess threw her hands in the air in celebration and twirled around. They had gone several hours without one creepy incident. Perhaps, they had just found themselves in a bad part of the woods, an area near some ancient burial grounds or a cursed plot of land.

Aiden and Tess walked beside the creek, following each dip and curve. The stream bubbled along as it flowed in the opposite direction. A fog hung over the water, obscuring its surface.

When they rounded a bend, the outline of a building came into view. Excitement rose in Tess's heart, then was promptly stamped out by her previous experience.

"Do you see it?" Tess asked, incredulity in her voice.

"I see it. It's there," Aiden reassured.

A smile crept across Tess's face as they neared the cabin. The dread stalking her since she arrived seemed to melt away. She scanned the cabin, noting all the windows in sight seemed intact; the building looked material and sturdy.

A low growl drew her attention away, and she froze. Aiden paused just behind her. A small animal stood on lowered haunches just a few feet from them. A coyote, teeth bared, was ready to pounce.

"Shoo! Go! Get outta here!" Aiden shouted at the animal. White, frothy saliva dripped from its maw as it crept forward. Its small paws stepped with delicate precision, nails like blades digging into the dirt. A red, fiery shimmer passed across its eyes. Tess had not encountered much wildlife in her past, but never had she seen an animal's eyes radiate such vivid, bizarre shades.

Tess stepped backward until she bumped into Aiden. The movement stirred the animal into action, and it sprinted towards them. Aiden pulled Tess by the arm, and they ran.

Avoiding falling into the creek or smacking into trees slowed their retreat. The coyote snarled as it neared them. Aiden pushed, weaving Tess through the woods until she stumbled and fell to the ground. Aiden tripped over her, landing and rolling a few feet away. The coyote bit at Tess's ankles, and she kicked at the animal's snout. Aiden crawled toward the scuffle and grabbed its jaws.

Tess stared wide-eyed as Aiden struggled against the grip of the coyote. As it pushed forward, attempting to bite down, Aiden pulled its mouth open, putting resistance on its snout. Crimson spilled over fangs chiseled to sharp points. Beneath the blood, the coyote's teeth were rotten with decay. As Aiden struggled to keep hold, the animal's teeth cut into his fingertips.

"Tess! My bookbag. There's a gun!" Aiden shouted.

"What?" Tess had heard him, yet the rabid animal's fangs were growing and the eyes, they swirled with sinister colors and she was dazed by its appearance.

"My bookbag!" Aiden yelled. He managed to push the wild animal away from her legs, and she pulled them close to her body. Tess ripped open Aiden's zippered pack and rummaged until cold plastic met her fingers. Just as she held out the firearm to Aiden, the coyote reared back and lunged at her, jaws wide, teeth bared, and aimed at her throat. Aiden slammed his hand into the animal's mouth. Tess shrieked and squeezed her eyes shut, awaiting impact or the sounds of Aiden being ripped apart.

Moments passed. Only the trickling stream met her ears. When she opened her eyes, Aiden sat, eyes gaping and body frozen. Tess twisted around, her gaze darting from place to place, expecting to see the vicious creature. The coyote was gone.

Tess reached her hand out to Aiden's shoulder. His gaze was fixed on his shredded arm.

"Are you okay?" Tess asked. He turned to her, his face pale and taut with worry.

"I'm okay. Are you?" Aiden inspected her ankle where the animal had been tearing the fabric.

"I'm fine. Did you see where it went?"

He shook his head. Aiden helped Tess to her feet. As she calmed her quaking body, she looked around the woods, anticipating reddish-brown fur or fangs. Only leafy oaks and pale birch trees gazed back at her.

"Well, the cabin is still there. That's a good sign," Aiden remarked.

"Let's get in there and patch you up." Tess hooked her arm in his and strode toward the cabin. As they walked along the side of the building, Tess repeatedly cast her eyes at the wooden siding to reassure herself it had not vanished. They stepped onto the porch, which housed a wooden swing and a worn welcome mat. Finally, here they were. The cabin was within reach—comforts and safety, and a roof over their heads.

Aiden gripped the doorknob and turned it, only to find the cabin locked.

6

RING, RING. THE '90s
ARE CALLING

"There's probably a key hidden out here somewhere. Didn't they email you instructions?" Aiden asked, flipping the welcome mat over to look underneath, revealing only broken leaves and dirt.

"Yeah, probably. In fact, let me check right now. Oh, *wait*. I can't," Tess scoffed, her response causing Aiden's face to fall. "I'm sorry. I just can't believe I smashed my phone!"

"So, you didn't memorize the email with instructions." Aiden maintained a solemn face until Tess cocked her head at him with a flustered smile. A laugh burst from him. "It's okay. We'll search for the key for a bit, but I'm not opposed to just breaking a window."

The pair searched the outskirts of the house, lifting flower pots and looking beneath nearby rocks. They tried door handles and tested windows for any that might be unlocked. After what felt like a thorough search, Tess sighed.

"Ready to break that window?" she asked.

Aidan ran his fingers through his hair as his eyes panned the home. "I guess there's no other option."

He picked up a rock the size of his hand and bashed it into a small panel of glass that bordered the front door. The shards rained down inside the home. Aiden reached a hand through, twisted the lock on the front door, and the two entered.

A musty cedar scent greeted Tess at the front door, reminding her of shop class back in high school—dust and freshly-cut wood. To be surrounded by walls and furniture was a comfort compared to the expanse outside. The enclosure made her feel secure. The home's decor was typical of a rented cabin: cedar furniture, faux taxidermy on the walls, and plaid rugs. Plush leather recliners called to her aching back and feet.

"Let's get your arm cleaned and covered."

Aiden removed the first aid kit from his pack and handed it to Tess. After sterilizing the rips and tears in Aiden's arm, she wrapped it with gauze and taped it.

Aiden closed and locked the front door. He scrutinized the area while Tess plopped down into a recliner that enveloped her body. She watched as Aiden investigated every surface, opening drawers and cabinets.

He swiped his finger across the kitchen counter and eyed the coating of dust. "Don't these places usually have cleaning crews?"

Tess shrugged. "It's probably in the email."

Aiden smirked at her as he rifled through a kitchen drawer. He set a hammer on the counter, then produced a roll of duct tape. His shoes crunched on splinters of glass as he approached the broken window. After ripping strips of tape from the roll, he placed them beside each other, covering the hole in the glass. Once the window was sealed, Aiden pressed a hand to the wall of tape, testing its strength.

"You're probably going to lose your security deposit." Aiden gestured to the makeshift repair job and tossed the duct tape roll on an end table between the recliners.

Tess's laugh came out strained, and she pushed a hand to her forehead. "What a nightmare." Then, she had an idea. Her head shot up, and she looked at Aiden with excitement in her eyes.

"Do you think this place has a home phone?" she asked.

"Oh, that's right. Landlines did exist at one time, didn't they?"

In unison, they stalked into the kitchen and perused the walls.

"Here!" Aiden shouted, and they rushed to the far wall. A beige phone hung in a cradle secured to the log siding. Tess picked it up and listened for a dial tone. There was a sound coming through. Not the dull tone of a phone awaiting a number to be dialed. Static. Except the static was intermittent, almost like the whirring of helicopter blades. Tess pressed buttons on the number pad, but no sounds indicated her actions. The whirring continued.

"What? Anything?" Aiden asked impatiently.

Tess shook her head and hung up the phone.

"Here, let me try." Aiden moved in and put the phone to his ear. His face scrunched in confusion. He tried pressing numbers, and must have received the same result because he hung the phone up shortly after.

Aiden grimaced. The pair returned to the comfort of the recliners and sat in silence.

"That coyote...it definitely had rabies, right?" Aiden asked.

Tess opened her mouth to spew details about its fangs, those mystical, dreadful eyes. There was no way to bring that up without sounding insane.

"I don't think I've ever seen an animal with rabies, but yeah, I guess it did."

Aiden stared blankly at the floor. "And then it just disappeared...after trying to rip me to shreds." Aiden held his arm up.

"Thank you, by the way," Tess said quietly.

"For?" Aiden cast her a puzzled look.

"That thing...the coyote was coming straight for my throat."

"Oh, no problem." Aiden looked away as though embarrassed.

Tess stared at him for a while. She wanted to ask, even though it was none of her business. There was not much to do here at the cabin but ruminate and entertain curiosity.

"Aiden, why do you have a gun?"

Aiden drew in a deep breath and bit his lower lip. "I...brought it for protection."

Tess furrowed her brows and aimed a penetrating stare at him. "Protection against what?"

Aiden ran his fingers through his hair and cradled his head, eyes cast down. "I really did come out here to reminisce, spend some time where my family shared some of our happiest memories."

Tess softened her expression, giving Aiden time to collect his thoughts.

"Shortly after I became a firefighter, my parents were in a fatal crash. I worked the scene. It was really bad. After their death, my sister came out here to, I don't know, clear her head. She ended up going missing. I spent a lot of time searching for her. At first, with the whole department, the sheriff's office, and the residents of the town. People slowly started to lose hope, and after a while, I was the only one who cared. Until even I gave up."

"They never found a body or anything?" Tess asked.

Aiden shook his head.

"I came out here to...I just, I don't have anyone left. Being in these woods was supposed to remind me of the good times, and I only felt lonelier. I really did bring the gun for protection."

Tears threatened to spill from Tess's lids. All the phone calls and visits with her mother that she took for granted—she could not imagine a world without her. Though she should be preparing her heart for that scenario.

Tess pictured her mom's smile that shone bright despite struggling through life with a deadbeat ex-husband and several bouts of cancer. Just before Tess had left to come on this trip, her mother had told her that she would have to go back to chemo. Tess tried to cancel her trip to be with her, but her mother had insisted Tess enjoy her time away. It was only a weekend, after all.

"I'm sorry, Aiden." The words came out choked.

Aiden rubbed tears from his eyes. "Don't be. There's a reason for everything, I guess."

The silence in the room grew tense as Tess sat with Aiden's heavy confession. Her thoughts raced with things to change the subject without seeming insensitive. Nothing came to mind.

"Maybe there's another landline upstairs?" Aiden asked, patting his knees and standing. Tess followed him to the base of the stairs and peered upwards. An ombre of shadows crept up the stairs until the upper floor disappeared into darkness.

"I'm sure it's a typical layout. Bedrooms. Bathroom. Maybe a linen closet," Tess said.

Aiden looked to her and cocked an eyebrow.

"Well, I'm going up to check it out. You can stay down here if you want. Alone."

Tess huffed. "Ready when you are."

Aiden smirked at her before heading up the stairs. Once at the landing, they scanned the hall, deciding which of the three closed doors to investigate first. Aiden headed towards the closest door, opened it slowly, and revealed another rustic-themed room. Aiden walked past the twin-sized bed to search around a roll-top desk, lifting the creaky cover to find only a bare surface.

Tess pushed into the room and opened up an oak wardrobe. Plastic hangers hung from a metal bar, and the scent of mothballs assaulted her nose.

The door slamming shut caused Tess to jump. Her wide eyes darted to Aiden, whose gaze was fixed on the room's entrance. He strode with intent until his hand gripped the doorknob and pulled. The door stayed shut.

"Is it locked?" Tess asked.

Aiden only shot her a solemn look and tugged at the door again.

"Aiden, open the door!"

"It won't budge."

Something heavy slammed against the door on the other side, and the pair jumped back.

Aiden crept toward the door again, hand out and ready to try the knob, when the impact occurred once more. Lowering his hand, Aiden backed away. Whatever was on the other side threw itself against the door over and over again until the two of them were huddled in a corner. Wood splintered as the door threatened to give way.

Tess's heart palpitated in frantic rhythms. Her mind scrambled to come up with possibilities as to what was on the other side of the door. Wood shards flew into the room as the door disintegrated against the force. Aiden shielded Tess's body with his arms, burying his face in her hair. They remained still, waiting to be torn apart.

Tess kept her eyes squeezed shut until she felt Aiden move. When she looked up, he was gazing at the doorway with a baffled expression. Tess followed his gaze to find the same perplexity. The doorway was empty. Other than the shredded wood, the bedroom was just as they had first found it.

7

HAUNTED

Aiden helped Tess to her feet. She pretended not to notice the way his arms shook. In silence, they moved out of the bedroom and back down the stairs. The recliners brought them minimal comfort as they attempted to relax, moving on as though nothing out of the ordinary had occurred. Tess sat, her back tense and breathing rigid, wanting to ask about the terrifying incident. However, speaking of it would confirm the disturbing reality of the situation.

After a while, Aiden stood and rummaged through the kitchen cabinets. He sifted and scrounged as Tess stared at the floor's hardwood planks.

Something was wrong with this place. She dared not call it *haunted*. That term was for cheesy houses filled with sound effects and people jumping out in masks. Tess was never a fan of horror; her own life met those needs when it came to the traumatic. Never before had she experienced the paranormal. No ghost sightings or objects moving on their own. The events here in this forest felt so surreal that she was certain she was a part of one of those prank shows and Aiden was an actor being paid to go along with all of it.

Tess eyed him warily as he made his way from the kitchen to sit beside her, offering a bag of tortilla chips that were sure to be stale. Nevertheless, she accepted the bag, desperate for something to eat, and scarfed down several chips. *Definitely* stale.

Guilt consumed Tess for her suspicions. Aiden was enduring the same unexplained phenomena and proving to be helpful and protective. He was another lost soul, vying for respite from life's crushing weight.

The pair munched on chips for a while, silently contemplating their predicament. Tess felt she was nearly ready to voice her fears and thoughts when a ringing sound erupted throughout the room. The unmistakable cheery tones of a phone call echoed around them.

"Where is that coming from?" Tess stood, glancing from table to table.

"Over here, I think," Aiden said, moving toward the kitchen. The pair crept across the floor, scanning wildly for the source of the high-pitched tones.

When she spotted it, Tess's heart seized up. The ringing did not just belong to a phone, but *her* phone, sitting on a side table near the back door. The screen lit up with her company's logo, and her boss's name was displayed at the top.

"No, how did it..." Tess trailed off as her eyes glazed over, staring at the device.

"Decline the call and see if you can try 911 again," Aiden said.

Tess's hands trembled as she picked up the phone she smashed just a day ago. She pressed her thumb to the red decline button. Instead of the call disappearing, a timer began, and her boss's voice emanated through the speaker.

"Tess! What the hell are you doing? Where are you? It's been weeks, and all your deadlines have passed due. I have lawyers up my ass, not to mention the damn media!"

Tess held the phone out as though it were a hot coal. "I didn't answer it. I tried to decline it!"

"I know," Aiden took the phone from her and tried ending the call. Jacob's voice continued to shout, berating and degrading Tess in every possible way. Aiden smashed his thumb against the end call button over and over, anger building with each touch. Finally, the phone hung up the call, and silence met them once more.

Aiden opened the dial pad and as he pressed the nine key, the phone exploded with notifications—emails, text messages, and voicemails. Ignoring the barrage of pings, he continued dialing. The phone made no attempt to connect his call, returning only dead air.

The flood of notifications continued, and Tess let out a furious growl. She moved in to take the phone from Aiden's hand, but he pushed past her and set the phone on the counter. He picked up the hammer he had left there and bashed the blunt end of it into the phone's screen until the light died out and the chimes cut short.

"That phone wasn't real. It had to be a trick. I saw you break it," Aiden said, leaning against the counter, panting.

"Did he say I've been gone for *weeks*?"

Aiden shook his head. "It's a trick. I'm telling you. It wasn't real."

Tess let out a shaky sigh. Evening was dipping into nighttime, the trees surrounding the cabin cast an ominous shadow across the home. She returned to the recliner and wrapped her arms around her knees. With a stern frown sewn on his lips, Aiden paced the kitchen floor.

"What's the plan?" Tess asked.

Aiden glanced up at her, his frown dissolving into surprise as though he had forgotten she was there. "I guess we'll stay the night here and continue on in the morning."

"Stay here? What about that thing upstairs?"

"Tess, *things* are happening to us everywhere. Inside, outside. At least in here we won't wake up with back pain."

Tess found a linen closet in the hall and retrieved two blankets. She tossed one to Aiden, who sat in the recliner beside hers, rocking his feet back and forth. Tess curled up in the leather chair, deploying the footrest, and covered herself in the plaid throw.

"Is your boss really like that?" Aiden asked, offering a saddened expression.

"Unfortunately," Tess replied, a tightness in her voice as she recalled the incessant shouting.

"That's a lot to deal with."

Tess shrugged. It was a lot. Thinking about it now left her depleted. Her legs ached from miles of walking. Fear still traversed her veins, leaving her weak and dizzy. Fragments of responses billowed up like bubbles in a pond, then faded away just as quickly. Her eyes drooped, and her head sagged against the tufted headrest. Within minutes, she was asleep.

8

HI, MOM

The sun glared through the living room windows, piercing Tess's eyes. She blinked away the fog of sleep, then sat up with a jolt. Her head swiveled around the room. Aiden lay stretched out on the recliner, breathing heavily, still in deep sleep. The counters were bare, save for the hammer and smashed phone, the furniture was still in its place—everything as it was when she closed her eyes for the night.

Rather than comfort her, this knowledge stirred suspicion. Whatever was feeding off of their fear must have been satisfied enough to leave them alone for a few hours.

Tess rose and stepped past Aiden toward the bathroom. At first, her steps were cautious so as not to disturb his sleep. His unconsciousness left her feeling alone. While she did not stomp down the hall, she resumed a normal gait.

When Tess returned, Aiden was sitting up in the recliner, rubbing his eyes.

"Good morning," he murmured.

"Nothing crazy happened last night, so I guess it is good."

Tess filled a glass with water from the sink and sipped it as she considered their next steps. "Don't suppose there's a map around here, do you?"

Aiden stretched his body out, his back and the joints in his knees popping. "I hope so. We can snoop around."

The pair got to work, opening drawers, sifting through cabinets, and searching tabletops. When Tess opened a coat closet near the front door, a horrid stench assaulted her nostrils. She grimaced and squinted her eyes. The odor relented a bit with the door ajar, and Tess chanced a look inside. Dimly lit and small, the darkness painted most of the area. Tess leaned in, eye to eye with a wooden bar that spanned from wall to wall, coat hangers dangling from around it.

As her eyes adjusted, she became aware of a long jacket hanging in the far corner, its color difficult to determine as it blended with the shadows. Something about the coat struck her as odd. Rather than hanging loosely, it appeared... full.

Tess glanced around for a light switch, dread slithering into the pit of her stomach. Her fingers slid along the inside of the walls, searching for the familiar plastic. When she came up short, she sighed and returned her gaze to the closet. A string dangled from the center of the ceiling, leading up to a single, uncovered bulb.

Against her better judgment, Tess reached out for the string. It would have been so easy to shut the door on her curiosity and let the abomination remain a mystery, but Tess was never one to let things go.

She tugged the string, illuminating the closet, and immediately flung herself backward. The coat on the rack dangled from a hanger, and a head hung from its neck. Not just the head of someone she recognized, but someone she cherished. Her mother's face peered out at her with dead eyes, gore spilling from her mouth.

Tess stumbled to the floor, sobbing. She crab-walked toward the door and kicked it shut, then scrambled backward until she was pressed against the base of the coffee table.

"What is it? What happened?" Aiden rushed to her, glancing intermittently at the closet door.

Tess pressed a hand to her mouth and shook her head. "Another trick! Another horrible, stupid trick! I hate this place!" Her head dropped into her hands, which shook at her hairline as furious tears cascaded down her face.

The sound of the closet opening and closing only affirmed her declaration. Aiden found nothing disturbing inside. It had all been in her head.

Aiden sat beside her on the ground. Tess's sobs consumed the air until she drew in a deep breath, desperate to stabilize her emotions.

"What did you see?" Aiden asked, his voice low and gentle.

"It doesn't matter. It was fake. Like the phone, like the voices, like the blinking puddle. All fake!" Tess shouted.

"It wasn't *fake*. Whatever we're dealing with plays tricks on the mind. Those tricks feel very real."

"I just want to go home." Tess lifted her head. Rivers of tears flowed down her cheeks. She clenched her fists, summoning the resolve to focus on the endgame.

"Let's keep looking for a map." Aiden stood and held a hand out to her. "We'll stick together this time. Might not keep something from happening, but at least we won't be alone."

Tess took his hand and rose. With the back of her hand, she wiped tears from her face. They continued their search, moving through every crevice of the living room and the bathroom until they reached an office at the end of the hall.

Tess fingered the spines of books on a shelf while Aiden sifted through papers in a desk drawer.

"Here!" Aiden called, pulling a map from a pile of papers and slamming it down on the desk. The front declared it was a map of Sacred Valley and its surrounding regions, including Sinner's Pass to the west and the town of Still Waters to the south. Aiden unfolded the map, laying it across the desk.

"Here's Sacred Valley," he pointed to a small town just north of the forest. Then, he circled a large area denoted by dark green shades. "We're...somewhere here in the Wilted Pines."

"Wilted Pines? How fitting," Tess commented. "Can you at least narrow down the general area of where we are?"

Aiden's finger trailed a thin ribbon of blue that snaked through the Wilted Pines. "Here's the stream and....here's where I figure the cabin to be." Aiden tapped a portion at the center of the forest.

"So, it looks like if we follow the stream, we could come out to Sacred Valley?" Tess said in a voice tinged with hope.

"As the crow flies, yes, but we don't know how the terrain is or if any of the creek has dried up in areas. I don't even know which direction is north."

"Can't you look at moss on trees and follow the North Star?"

Aiden laughed. "Sure, Bear Grylls. Or we can see where the sun sets tonight. That should give us an idea."

Tess groaned. "I miss GPS."

9

THEY'RE JUST TREES

"We're *really* going to spend another night here?" Tess complained.

"It's not ideal, but unless you have a compass hidden somewhere, I'd rather not start off in a direction that leads us away from town."

Tess sat back hard against the recliner and sighed. Her stomach let out a ferocious growl.

"I'm starving," she complained. Aiden nodded in agreement, glancing around the home in a half-hearted attempt. The truth was, they had picked the downstairs clean, and the chances of finding food upstairs were slim.

This would not abide. Tess would not sit idly waiting for her stomach to cave in on itself with hunger. She stood with intent, approached the stairs, and gripped the handrail. After a deep intake of breath, she climbed.

"What are you doing?" Aiden asked from behind her.

"I doubt there's any food up here, but I have to be sure."

The walk up felt like it took an eternity. Tess's hands clutched the rail with excessive strength, the previous day's fright fresh in her mind. At the top, she cast a hesitant glance to the right. The bedroom remained in disarray, a scene frozen in time from their last venture into it. Splinters of wood littered the floor, and fragments of the door hung from the hinges.

Dim light washed over the hall, with only one window at the far left end letting in light. A door stood directly in front of her, innocuous, dormant. A chill swept across her forearms, causing the hairs to raise. Tess swore that the temperature had dropped considerably, but chalked it up to her fear.

After burying the instinct to retreat down the stairs, Tess opened the door. Movement inside caused her to flinch until she realized it was the opening door reflected in a mirror. As the door swung, Tess named the objects as they became visible. Sink. Toilet. Bath rug. Shower curtain.

The curtain was pale yellow, covered in swirls of daisies. Meant to be pleasant, but Tess knew better. The ominous shower curtain was hiding something. They always were. Her brows furrowed, and she steeled herself, fists clenching in preparation. On feet reluctant to move, Tess stepped into the bathroom. Her hand quaked as she neared the tub.

With her eyes intently fixed on the patterned daisies, Tess's vision began to blur. The tips of her fingers grazed the fabric. Her thoughts pummeled her with all the things she could find behind the curtain—a psychotic killer ready to stab her, a pile of dead bodies, the coyote ready to lunge for her throat.

"Find anything? I couldn't let you have all the fun up here by yourself." Aiden's voice sent a jolt through her heart. Her head whipped toward him as he entered the bathroom. Though she could not see herself, Tess was sure the color had drained from every part of her body.

"What is wrong with you?" Tess gasped, both hands covering her chest where her heart thrummed frantically.

"I didn't mean to scare you. I didn't realize you were...what *are* you doing?"

"It's stupid, but I just had to check behind the—" Tess turned back to the tub, and the terror, just starting to wane, overtook her once more. The shower curtain was wide open. Rather than staring at pale yellow and white flowers, the tub gaped at her, empty except for a water ring around the rim.

"Did you...I didn't..."

"Tess, what's wrong?" Aiden asked.

She simply shook her hand. The uncertainty felt like mad tendrils waving about in her mind, crashing into everything she thought to be real. The important thing was that nothing sinister dwelled behind the curtain. For now, at least.

"Let's just check the other rooms."

The pair moved on, entering the final room. This one was expansive with a sprawling king-sized bed, matching armoires, and an armchair that faced a bay window. Tess pushed the frilly blue curtains aside to reveal the creek, winding around from the backside of the cabin and further into the forest.

The woods were speckled with a mixture of gaunt trees and some that stood like fierce protectors of the dubious land. The luscious greenery contrasted with their bleak predicament. Tess was sure she would never look at a group of trees the same, forever suspicious of what tricks they might play on her. The ones here mocked her, looming towards the window, taunting her to try and escape.

They're just trees, Tess. Chill.

When she started to turn away, Tess caught a glimpse of something between two trees. A small flash of tan fur. She jerked her head back, expecting to see the coyote glaring up at her. Eyes dancing across the ground, Tess scanned the sprawling landscape only to find it empty as before.

"Well, no food in here," Aiden declared, shutting a door to an armoire. He came to stand beside Tess and drink in the view of the desolate forest. A deep sigh left his lips. Tess tried to imagine what he had gone through: losing his family, life crashing down around him, feeling bitter and hopeless. The pistol in his bag weighed heavy on her mind. For protection, he had claimed. She saw the determined sorrow in his eyes and was certain he had other plans for the gun.

Though their time together had been short, Tess found Aiden to be kind, encouraging, and unintentionally humorous; to deprive the world of this incredible being would have been a heinous tragedy. If that were not enough to appreciate his presence, it helped her immeasurably that he was here. Navigating this horrific forest alone would have diminished her sanity.

The pair returned to the comfort of the living room. Nothing menacing had occurred in this space, which created a sense of safety with Tess. The forest and its malevolent incidents seemed to have no explicit boundaries. Tess knew she was a fool to believe the living room was off-limits, like base in tag. Nevertheless, her worries felt lighter in the room.

Aiden paced the floor, the gentle tapping of his footfalls becoming a soundtrack to their unspoken plight. It had been half a day since they had eaten, and the sensation of hunger was already a clawing, desperate need.

The sound was subtle at first. Aiden's steps nearly drowned it out, except in an atmosphere with such little noise, it became evident immediately. Aiden paused, looking around, his eyes meeting Tess's every few seconds. She nodded, affirming she heard the sound, too. From a distance, the soft wail of a creature howling echoed through the woods.

10

AN APPLE A DAY

Aiden's face transformed from curiously in tune with the sound to determined anger as he ripped the pistol from his backpack. He stalked towards the back door.

Tess jumped up from her seat. "Wait, don't go out there! What if it's a trick?"

"It's just that damn coyote. I'm going to put an end to it."

Aiden pulled the door open, Tess following closely behind, and the pair stepped onto the back porch. The moment they entered the atmosphere outside, the air changed. As if they had fallen deaf, the world around them stilled—the coyote's cries swallowed by the twisted woods.

They peered around, the silence feeling pregnant with something treacherous.

"Look!" Aiden said, his voice overbearing in the dead air. He pointed to the creek's bank, lined with trees and thorn bushes. As Tess followed his directive, one tree in particular stood out. Bright, glossy leaves shone in what little sunlight the trees allowed through. Its small stature dwarfed it in comparison to the towering pines and gnarled oaks. Glistening red orbs clung to the end of nearly every branch.

"Are those apples?" Tess asked. Before she realized it, she was hurtling towards the tree. Aiden passed her quickly, the desperation obvious in his swift gait.

Aiden tugged one from a branch and bit into it. His face morphed into an expression of ecstasy. Tess chuckled as she pulled her own from the tree and turned to Aiden, prepared to extend a "cheers" for their serendipitous find. Juices spilled down his chin, and Tess's amused sentiment faded. She snatched the fruit from his hand and threw it to the ground along with her own.

"Another damn trick!" Tess wailed, swatting at Aiden's face.

Aiden deflected her attempts, then glanced down at the apples with horrified bewilderment. "What the hell did you do that for?"

"You didn't feel them?"

"Feel *what?*" Aiden's tone revealed that he had grown tired of her fearful outbursts.

"There were spiders. Like, a hundred of them!"

Aiden plucked another apple from the tree and withdrew a pocket knife, slicing the apple open. Spiders oozed from the fruit's core, dashing across the peel and over Aiden's hands as if vying for escape. Tess looked at Aiden expectantly, and he shrugged.

"Enjoy your apples," Tess said with contempt, and stomped back towards the cabin.

As she took her first step on the porch, the coyote's howl erupted throughout the woods—one sound seemingly everywhere at once. Tess turned to Aiden, eyes wide and breathing erratic. Aiden flipped the bottom of his shirt up into a makeshift basket and piled apples in until they were toppling out. Holding the shirt basket steady, he sprinted until he reached the cabin, and Tess closed the door behind him. She locked the door.

Aiden dropped the apples onto the counter while Tess found the safety of her recliner and curled into it. She ruminated over the events in the forest, the horrors shared between Aiden and her, and the things she seemed to conjure in her mind. Were there logical explanations for the shared events? The other occurrences, the ones experienced by her alone, seemed to be evidence that she was breaking.

"Tess, I didn't mean to snap at you back there. I was so freaking happy to finally find something to eat, so when you saw the... spiders, it was frustrating." Aiden sat in the recliner next to hers, eyes full of remorse.

Tess swiped a hand down her face, letting out an exasperated breath. "Maybe I *didn't* see them. Maybe I'm going insane!"

"I believe you saw them. This forest, it plays tricks on people. We've seen that..."

"You seem to know an awful lot about this forest." Tess eyed him, suspicions flooding her brain faster than she could comprehend.

"What does that mean?"

"Maybe YOU are playing tricks on people." Tess regretted the words the moment they left her lips. The accusation made no sense. Unless Aiden had this forest completely rigged with haunted house effects, and let a coyote tear up his arm to buy belief.

"Right," Aiden said, drawing out the single syllable. "I bashed the door to pieces upstairs while sitting right next to you. And crafted an iPhone from scratch, AND filled apples with spiders..."

Tess looked away from him, her body rigid with tension. She cowered at the conflict as shame washed over her. She was at work, being berated by her boss, Jacob, all over again. Except this interaction cut deeper, shame and embarrassment weighing heavy on her, because not only was she the one to forego the trust she had built, but Aiden was not cruel and insensitive like Jacob; he was patient and caring.

"Look, I shouldn't have yelled. I know this forest has us all twisted up. I'm just gonna leave you alone for a little while."

Tess listened as Aiden's footsteps retreated from her. A door opened, and she imagined he escaped into the office where they had found the map.

It was like her to lash out in tense moments.

Tess thought back to a particular lunch outing with her mother. A few months had passed since she had taken the job with Cypress Pharmaceuticals, and the pressure was already more than Tess could endure. With ease, her mother had suggested she find something else. Simple as that, right? Just put her two weeks in, and find another job. All of the training and fawning over the higher ups, the strife and late hours Tess had put in would have been in vain.

All of her mother's enthusiasm and support had shattered the moment Tess leaned forward, her face inches away from her mother's, and growled, "This is the real world, mom. I don't hide behind sunshine and rainbows like you. I can't just up and quit my job. Do you even hear yourself?"

Tess had watched the words crash into her mother, leaving her crestfallen and fighting back tears. She had seen a similar look the moment she accused Aiden of deception. Agonizing guilt crushed her.

With her arms wrapped around her legs and her head resting atop her knees, Tess wept.

11

Got Any Twos?

T he day carried on with Tess tucked into her leather safety net. Occasionally, she would hear movement from the office, imagining Aiden rifling through papers or sifting through drawers. The apples sat on the granite countertop. She knew they were just as they were when Aiden brought them in, but she swore they looked redder, appeared juicier. She longed for a taste.

Tess stood and made her way to the kitchen. She eyed the apples with suspicion, awaiting the tiny arachnid legs to poke through. She took a knife from the block beside the stove and readied herself for skittering spiders. The knife sliced through the apple's skin with ease, and to her surprise, only pale yellow fruit slick with moisture peeked out at her.

Tess picked up the apple, examined it one last time before sinking her teeth in. Bitter and sweet erupted on her tongue, almost too much to take after such little sustenance the past few days. Once she started, Tess was unable to quit. After several minutes, three apple cores stripped of their fruit sat on the counter.

She cast a glance toward the office door. The spiders, they had looked so real, scampering across the skin of the fruit and over the tops of Aiden's hand.

Tess grabbed an apple from the counter and made her way to the office. Apologies had never been her strong suit, even at work where she felt like she was groveling constantly. In fact, her relationship with her mother might not have filled her with so much shame had she spent more time learning how to say sorry.

This situation, to her chagrin, was more dire than a tiff with her mother. Steeped in necessity, her survival depended on it. Working with Aiden in harmonious tandem increased the chances of fleeing this damned place.

Tess's knuckles rapped gently on the door.

"Come in," Aiden said.

Tess pushed the door open, finding Aiden sitting in the office chair with his feet propped on the desk. An open book lay across his knees.

"What are you reading?" Tess asked.

Aiden looked at the book's cover. "It's just about plant life in the area. I don't know. I was just flipping through it."

Tess nodded. "I'm sorry about earlier. I brought you an apple."

Aiden's eyes widened. "No more spiders?"

Tess shook her head. Aiden smiled and accepted her apology apple. He bit into it and sighed in delight.

"I don't blame you for earlier, by the way. Honestly, I'd be concerned if you didn't suspect me."

"How long have you been here, anyway?" Tess asked, relieved that Aiden held no grudge against her.

Aiden shrugged, chewing another bite of apple. "A few days that have felt like a few years."

Tess studied him. His demeanor toward the forest seemed to match hers: uncertain, terrified, and unprepared for the next scare. Though there was a calm aura about him, as though some part of him had come to expect the horrors. Perhaps not everyone was as high-strung as she was.

"Check this out," Aiden said, finishing the last bite of fruit and tossing the core into a small, metal trash bin. He stood and pulled something small from the top of the bookshelf: a dusty blue set of playing cards.

"Up for a round?"

Tess laughed nervously. "A round of what?"

"Anything. What's your game?" Aiden slid the cards from the cardboard box and began shuffling them.

"I'm not much of a card player."

"You know the rules for Go Fish?" Aiden bridged the cards between his fingers, sending them shooting between each other in a crisp shuffle.

"I mean... I haven't played since I was in elementary school."

"Go Fish it is," Aiden said, dealing them each a hand of cards. "You go first."

Tess eyed him incredulously, then sighed. Sure. They had hardly eaten, barely knew each other, and were trapped in a forest that had something terribly wrong with it. *Playing Go Fish is totally appropriate.*

Tess looked through the cards in her hand, hoping she had been dealt a pair already. No such luck. "Got any... eights?"

Aiden rifled through his hand, then smirked. "Nope! Go fish."

Tess picked up a card from the deck that lay face down on the desk and added it to her hand.

"My turn. Got any queens?" Aiden asked.

Tess shook her head. "Go fish."

Aiden drew a new card. "So, when you're not exploring haunted landscapes, or working a toxic job, what do you spend your time doing?"

"I need a two. And... I don't know. Fall asleep to cheesy movies and go shopping for things I convince myself are luxuries, if wearing clothes newer than five years old can be considered luxuries," Tess answered.

"No twos. Self-care is pretty much your strong point, then? And give me an eight."

"Self-care wound me up here. I already asked *you* for an eight. Are you cheating?" Tess glowered at Aiden, watching his face transform into fearful confusion.

"Wait, I didn't have this before. How...ugh. I hate this place." Aiden handed over the eight in his hand.

Tess smiled triumphantly, laid the pair of eights down, and looked through her hand. "How about a seven? What kind of music do you like?"

Aiden paused, considering his cards. "Go fish. A little bit of everything, but mostly country. And, king?"

"Go fish, cowboy. I need...a queen," Tess said.

"I don't have any. You already—damnit. Here you go," Aiden handed her the card.

"You know, maybe we had this forest figured all wrong. It's just a lonely spirit, waiting for two people to play Go Fish beneath its glorious tree branches." The grin on Tess's face was relentless. Aiden only stared at her, his lips set in a straight line.

"Go again, tree whisperer."

"Let's see. How about a ten?"

"Nope. But I'll take that two off your hands." It was Aiden's turn to grin. Tess handed the card over reluctantly.

"Wait, did you pick that up from the deck?" Tess asked.

"Don't worry. I picked it up last round."

Tess smiled and continued the game. "Favorite movie?"

"This might surprise you, but I'm kind of a Star Wars guy."

"That doesn't surprise me in the least."

Aiden scrunched his brows. "Why doesn't that surprise you?"

Tess asked for a card, which Aiden gave reluctantly, then shrugged. "I just mean... lots of people like Star Wars."

Tess turned down Aiden's request for a card, and he drew from the pile.

"There was something *personal* about your statement. I heard it in your voice."

Tess laughed and shook her head. "Fine, you seem like a Star Wars kind of guy. Smart, *very* nice, and kind of...nerdy."

"Nerdy?!" Aiden held his hands out and looked himself over. Tess covered her face with the hand of cards, giggling behind them. Aiden's mouth hung open at her revelation, yet the corners of his mouth inched into a grin. "Nerdy. Wow. Okay, your favorite movie. Go."

After giving Aiden a matching pair, Tess pursed her lips. "You're going to make fun of me."

"Good! I need some material. I'm getting slaughtered in the game, and my self-esteem has really taken a hit!"

"The Devil Wears Prada," Tess answered.

"My sister loved that movie."

"What's not to love?" Tess asked. "Ruthless career moves, power, fashion."

"And you're officially more terrifying than this forest."

12

THE DOOR

After fifteen or more rounds of Go Fish, Tess and Aiden polished off the remaining apples and settled in for the night. They experienced several more instances of their cards being switched around, mostly in Tess's favor, and they were pleased not to experience the forest's more horrific antics. The break gave them time to breathe and bond; it almost felt relaxing.

Whatever inhabited these woods had a knack for playing tricks on the mind. Other than the coyote, most of the occurrences were harmless. Tess pondered again if the coyote was real rather than a deception. Perhaps this was all a game of survival. If she and Aiden could outsmart the woods without being distracted by the constant misdirection, they could find their way out.

Her mind fogged over as sleep took hold. Thunder roared, shaking the cabin to the foundation. Tess jolted awake and sat up in a panic. Darkness hung heavy over the room, thick like a blanket. Tess tried to peer through the black at Aiden. His features were obscured, slowly coming into focus, and she flinched when his eyes were fixed on her until she realized he was doing the same as her: waiting for the dark to wane to see if she was awake.

"You okay?" Aiden asked.

Tess nodded, then understood how dumb that was, considering he probably could not see her. "Yeah, I'm fine. Grateful we're in the cabin since it sounds like it's about to downpour."

"Agreed."

Thunder rumbled, low and angry, echoing around the cabin. The sound surrounded them like a predator, stalking them, toying with them. Lighting cracked against a tree nearby, sending a ripple of trembling through the house and illuminating the cabin in a blinding glow that was gone just as swiftly as it came.

Small droplets of rain began pattering against the roof. Tess wrapped her arms around her knees as she listened. There was something wrong about the way the rain sounded when it connected overhead.

A roar tore through the woods once more, thunder snapping like bones. The downfall swelled until it pelted the roof with force. Window panes rattled as a fierce gale swept against the home. A brilliant flash lit up the cabin and the area outside the windows, revealing a dense steam that had moved in on them.

"Do you hear that?" Aiden asked. Tess knew he meant the rain, the way it sizzled when it met the roof. She also knew he did not expect her to provide an answer.

The pair sat huddled in the living room, helpless to only listen to the storm rage outside. Each time the lightning erupted, unveiling their surroundings, Tess expected some devastating and horrific revelation. Every ripple of thunder felt as though it were crawling beneath her skin.

A water droplet fell onto Tess's forearm. Instinctively, she looked upward, though it was too dark to see the ceiling. As the drop trickled down her skin, a searing pain trailed in its path. She swiped away the water, only to feel a burn on her palm where she touched it.

Another drop landed, catching her flesh on fire. She dabbed at the liquid with her shirt and jumped to her feet.

"What is it?" Aiden asked. "Ow!"

The recliner rocked back and forth as Aiden ejected himself from it. His frenzied movements mimicked Tess's as they danced around in agony.

The cabin hissed as the acidic rain drenched everything around them. Tess's eyes stung as fog rose up from the floor, and she realized that materials around the house were smoking. When a flash of lightning flickered, Tess looked up and saw azure, cloudy sky through corroded holes in the ceiling.

As more droplets sizzled on her skin, she rushed to the closet, ignoring the possibility that her dead mother would still be hanging from a coat hanger. She ripped two rain coats from the rack, covered herself, and pushed the other into Aiden's hands.

"This won't hold up, but it'll buy us some time. Can you hold it over me? I have an idea." Aiden swiped the hammer from the kitchen counter and headed toward the back of the house. As Tess followed him, haphazardly holding both coats above them, lancing pain heated her exposed fingers. Aiden paused in the living room to toss his bag around his shoulders. They stopped at the office door, and Aiden tapped at the hinges with a hammer and his pocket knife. One by one, the pins from the hinges fell to the floor.

Tess chanced a glance behind them. If the dark were not enough to blind her, the rising smoke clouded the area even more. A flicker of lightning showed that the rain had begun to destroy the floor, and it was only a matter of time before they would fall through.

Another thud against the wood floor, and the door was free from its frame. Aiden caught the door before it fell to the ground. His breathing was labored, and Tess shuddered to imagine what his flesh had endured.

Together, they picked up the door and held it over them. The corrosive rain fell, and the wood immediately started to sizzle. In tandem, they walked through the living room. Aiden knocked his foot into the coffee table and let a surprised yelp. Once at the front door, Aiden jutted his hand out, turned the slick knob, and thrust the door open. They tilted their overhead protection to fit through and exited the cabin.

13

BLINDING LIGHTS

Once out of the house, the walls groaned and snapped as they gave way to the acid's destructive effects. Their steps were slow and measured as they walked through the dense forest. The tips of Tess's fingers were numb, and she was certain there were no layers of skin left. As she pressed her palms against the underside of the door, she could feel warm blood trickling down her arm.

The storm swelled, and every few seconds lightning stabbed downward, followed by bone-rattling thunder. As they pressed on, parts of the door became spongy, and they had to readjust their hold. The acrid smell of burnt paint overwhelmed Tess's senses. The laminate popped overhead as the rain sizzled through it.

Tess felt a crack snaking through the wood beneath her hand.

"It's not going to hold! We need to find cover!" she yelled up to Aiden. He said nothing and kept moving. A corner of the door near Tess fell away, exposing her shoulder to the acidic downpour. She tucked her shoulder in so that it was beneath what was left of the shield.

The door rocked back and forth as Aiden shuffled his hands into a new position, covering the parts of him that had been exposed.

If they did not find permanent cover, they were going to die.

A pulse of lightning set the world around them aglow for a mere second. If Tess's eyes had not been set in a certain direction, she would have missed it—a rock overhang tucked into the ground.

"There!" she shouted. Aiden stopped to look around, but there was no time. Tess shoved the door from their hands, grabbed the fabric of his coat, and pulled him beneath the rock. Their backs slammed into the stone wall, the overhang just barely covering their feet.

Panting and trembling, the pair sat watching the rain drop and sizzle against the dirt. As if defeated, the storm slowly ebbed, the rain died to a soft mist, and the lightning and thunder.

"Are you okay?" Tess asked, unsettled by the long silence they had fallen under.

"I...I'm still here. That's...something," Aiden replied.

"How bad are your burns?" In the reprieve, Tess's fear had faded, allowing the burning agony of every raindrop that had touched her skin to light her flesh on fire.

"I won't know until I can see but it's...bad."

"Aiden, I want to go home. I want to see my mom again. I want to eat at that little cafe on the street corner we go to on Saturday mornings. I think I wouldn't even mind seeing my boss at this point."

Tess awaited a chuckle or a snarky response.

"I know. I want to go home, too." The hope in him had fizzled out, just as swiftly as the storm had departed. It left Tess feeling doomed. She closed her eyes and leaned her head on Aiden's shoulder, exhaustion taking hold after their narrow escape.

The music was soft at first. Tess guessed the song had wormed its way into her brain, the way music often does. A word or a note reminds the subconscious of a familiar song and from then on, it plays repeatedly in one's mind. When she tried to focus on a different song, the music swelled, drifting from somewhere out in the woods.

Tess lifted her head from Aiden's shoulder to gaze out from the stone overhang. Darkness pierced her eyes as she strained them to see. The volume increased until it sounded as if the song were coming from within the cave.

"Is that the Weeknd?" Aiden asked.

"Yeah," Tess whispered, though she was not certain why she felt the need to keep her voice down.

"At least the forest has good taste." He propped his head back against the rock, clearly unbothered by another delusion.

Tess settled back, listening as Blinding Lights continued playing. The song ended and started again. Ire built up in her chest, burning rage against the forest and its deceptions—the way it belittled her at every turn. Each mind game was an opportunity for this wasteland to prove how pathetic and small she was. Each event, a test of her sanity, a play at her intelligence.

The upbeat tempo blared in her ears. Tess knew the words by heart. It was the song that was playing on her car stereo when she turned off the engine and headed into the woods to look for a secluded cabin.

14

THE ESCAPE PLAN

When Tess opened her eyes, the sun had lit up the forest. A lazy, yellow haze washed over the trees, producing vivid greens and rich browns. The way the woods sat still and majestic after the previous night's events was like someone who had just committed a discreet crime, then carried on through their day as if nothing were out of the ordinary. It frustrated Tess, made her feel crazy.

She turned to Aiden and sucked in a sharp breath at the sight of him. His face was mottled with pink, raw blotches where the rain had hit him. The caustic liquid had chewed through his clothes in patches; some of the affected fabric was rimmed red with blood.

"Aiden," Tess whispered. "Wake up."

His eyes fluttered behind his lids at the sound of her voice. When he opened them, they were bloodshot. As Aiden's eyes took her in, Tess saw a flicker of terror that he promptly masked.

"What?" Tess asked. She looked down and gasped. The rain had eaten through parts of her shoes, the plastic of the laces melted into her skin. Her jeans had holes throughout, exposing bleeding skin between the charred edges. The sleeves of her shirt were nearly disintegrated, leaving oozing, raw flesh. She held up her hands, and a horrified scream escaped her.

The skin around her nails was blistered and peeling away with yellow liquid weeping from deep craters. Chunks of her fingertips were gone, leaving only fatty tissue hanging from them. In some places, white, glossy bone peeked through what was left of her flesh.

"Oh, God," Tess whimpered. "No, no, no. I can't do this. This place is going to kill us!" She held her mangled, quivering hands out in front of her.

"It's not going to kill us," Aiden said without emotion. "It's just going to make us *wish* we were dead."

"What do we do? How do we get out of here?!"

Aiden was quiet for a long time while Tess sobbed beside him. Then, he pulled the pack from around his shoulders and unzipped it.

"I won't let it go that far," he said, sifting through the bag. "I think we still have a chance, but just in case." Aiden lifted the gun out of his bag and held it up. "Before it goes too far, before this forest tortures us to an inch of our lives, I can end it."

Tess stared at the pistol in horror. The thought was absolutely insane. Tess would never kill herself. She looked down at her hands, the blackened, bloody gore, and was not sure how much more she could take. Nodding softly, she accepted that a bullet in the head might be the best possible outcome, and tears streaked her face.

Aiden's eyes pierced the weapon in his hand. "I can save us from this."

Aiden tended to Tess's tattered fingers: wiping away blood, clipping bits of dangling flesh, and wrapping the tips to maintain the use of her hands. They sat in silence a long time after, staring at the charred remnants of the wooden door that protected them all the way to the rock overhang.

"You don't happen to have the map still, do you?" Tess asked.

Aiden sifted through the contents of his pack until he pulled the folded map from it. When he opened it up, the inside was blank.

"Cool. That's helpful," Tess deadpanned.

"We can't be too far from the creek. If we can find it, we can follow it away from the cabin. It'll take us a little farther north than we need to go, but it'll get us there."

Tess opened her mouth to suggest that his plan would work only if the forest allowed. So far, the woods seemed to spin and contort to achieve its own sinister goals. She chose not to hurl unhelpful words. If he wanted to cling to false hope, Tess would let him.

"Sounds like a plan."

Aiden helped Tess to her feet, ducking beneath the overhang to emerge into the open. They spent a few moments glancing around, and Tess wondered if Aiden was noticing the same thing as her. The corroded door laid in pieces at their feet, but the forest seemed otherwise untouched by the acidic storm. Trees were intact, leaves were whole, the ground was impeccable aside from foliage that had fallen lazily to their deaths.

The pair had come from the right during the night. The left would lead away from the cabin and the stream, so they headed straight in search of the creek.

The air around them maintained a calm stillness. Every twig and leaf was in its place, yet Tess eyed it all with suspicion. Her stomach twisted in anticipation of some new, unknown horror.

The pain in her hands crawled up her arms like a constrictor tightening its grip. Her fingers trembled. She was glad they were covered and wondered how they would heal—if she would ever appear normal again.

"Favorite thing to eat?" Aiden asked, slicing through the bleak silence. Tess sighed. The prospect of light conversation felt too much for her weary brain.

"Pizza," she indulged him anyway. In truth, all she could think of was the personal Margherita pizzas she ordered every Saturday when she ate at the Toadhead Cafe with her mom. The tomatoes were always fresh, the slivers of mozzarella always creamy. "Yours?"

"Steak. A big, juicy, steak."

For several minutes after, their steps were the only sound.

"Boyfriend?" Aiden asked.

Tess cocked an eyebrow at him.

"What? Just making conversation."

Her gaze fused with the ground as she considered his question.

"No," she finally answered. "Never had much luck with relationships. Could be the toxic job. I don't know. They just never stick around for long."

"Sorry. It's hard to balance work *and* a love life. Or so I've heard."

"No girlfriend for you?" The moment the question escaped, a pang of guilt washed over her. Aiden had insinuated that he had meant to take his own life. Surely, there was no girlfriend in the mix.

"Na, I guess I'm too *nerdy*," Aiden laughed, a tinge of hollowness in his tone.

Tess offered a tight smile, her mind scrambling for new topics of conversation.

"Have you ever binge-watched an entire TV series in one day?"

When Aiden said nothing, Tess assumed he was pondering his answer, but when she looked over at him, his eyes were fixed toward something in the distance. She strained her eyes, looking between trees.

"Do you see—"

"Shh," Aiden cut her off. They stopped walking and listened.

"Do you hear that?" Aiden asked. Tess focused on the sounds around her, and shook her head.

"Come on," he instructed, and broke into a swift gait.

After traversing several feet, the sound hit her ears and it sounded glorious—the trickle of a stream.

Once their feet kissed the creek's bank, they broke left, steering clear of the muddy, eroded sides. Clear, sparkling water rippled across fallen branches and smooth rocks.

The sound of it was like something from a storybook, forged by God himself. The sun shined on the surface, casting a glare that lightened the dirt and leaves flanking it on either side.

They began a steady trek that paralleled the water, and though a quiet hope lingered between them, Tess could not help but feel that a looming dread slithered beneath it.

15

It's In The E-Mail

The afternoon gave way to evening. The creek wound left, then right, twisting and turning as it ran its deep gouge through the ominous forest. Tess shivered as the pain in her fingers grew to feel like thousands of needles digging into her skin. A constant ache consumed her feet as they padded along the ground. Various patches of skin, inflamed from the previous night's rain, left her in agony.

"Looks like there's something up ahead," Aiden remarked. The mere possibility of something different than tree after tree pushed them forward.

Aiden was right. In the distance, Tess could see the outline of something dark behind the trees. Something tall. A building. And as they approached, she recognized precisely what it was. Her heart sank.

The two trudged along the creek bank until they stood staring at the cabin. The same one they had escaped in the middle of the night. The exterior was intact, no signs of damage from the caustic precipitation.

Tess fell to her knees with her head in her hands.

"No, no, no, no, no," she muttered.

"Maybe...maybe it's a different cabin. They used the same floor plan and—"

"It's the same, stupid cabin!" Tess shouted. "We've been walking all day just to end up in the same place!"

"We knew this was a possibility—"

"We're never getting out of here," Tess whimpered.

Aiden fell to a sitting position beside her. "Tess, we have to keep moving. We'll find a way out, I promise."

"You can't promise that! You're just as hopeless as I am!"

The air around Tess thinned, and a deep moan bellowed through the trees. Yet again, Tess had let her emotions rule the situation. Rage rippled through her, and she attacked the one person helping her. Slivers of memories paraded through her mind, her mother pleading with her to quit her job, Tess shouting pathetic excuses. The fear of being unsuccessful morphed to anger that she directed at her mother constantly.

Aiden must have been hurt by her words because he had not said a single thing. Tess drew in a slow breath in preparation for her apology. She counted to ten, steadied her nerves, and lifted her head.

When she looked up, Aiden was nowhere to be seen. Only the cabin loomed over her, its mocking stance watching her realize she was alone.

"Aiden?" Tess called out. His name echoed off the trees back to her. She stood, eyes darting around in a frantic pattern. "Aiden?!"

He had just been right beside her. Talking. Breathing. *Hadn't he?*

She had been sitting there longer than she realized. That must have been it. Aiden probably decided to give her some space and went into the cabin. Tess glared at the cabin. The entire forest had proven to be nefarious, but the cabin had brought on the most intense situations. If Aiden was in there, Tess would muster the courage to enter.

She approached the same door she and Aiden had come to just a few days before. When she tried to turn the knob, it was locked.

A tense chuckle escaped her. "Key's probably mentioned in the email," she muttered. Admittedly, the rock she picked up offered no clear evidence that it was the same one Aiden had thrown through the window before, yet she felt in her core that it was. Pain surged through her as she gripped the rock. The tattered remnants beneath the wrappings burned from the contact with the stone's rough, jagged edges. Tess breathed in deeply, willing herself to ignore the pain.

With the window broken and the door unlocked, Tess entered. Silence swallowed her whole. The recliners were empty. Even the blankets they had slept beneath were nowhere in sight. No broken phone on the floor. No tools left out on the counter. It was as if her and Aiden had never been there at all.

On unsteady feet, Tess carried herself around the ground floor—everything like a still life, untouched by human hands. When she peered out the back door, she was not surprised to see the apple tree missing.

The office was desolate without Aiden's presence. Threads of memories flashed through her mind: the card game, the laughter. Tess noted the deck of cards sitting on the shelf under a layer of dust. She sighed and shut the door.

Aiden was not downstairs. Tess stood at the foot of the steps gazing into the black abyss of the upper floor. Everything in her being warned her against going up.

"Aiden?" she called, hoping he would answer, hoping he would prevent her from having to travel up the steps and into the petrifying atmosphere. None came.

The wood creaked beneath her as she ascended each stair, walking as if in slow motion. Her body tensed, awaiting a coyote howl or a ghost to fly down at her or spiders to crawl from the walls. Once at the top, Tess scanned the three doors, finding them intact. After building up her courage, she burst through each door, performed a quick search with her eyes, and shut the doors again.

Tess practically ran down the stairs once it was determined that Aiden was not on the upper floor.

The next several hours were spent sitting in the recliner, staring at the swirls in the wood grain floor, and shouting Aiden's name from the front and back door.

Of all the things encountered in this nightmarish patch of land, being alone was the worst, by far.

16

WAKE UP, TESS

Nighttime settled over the cabin. Tess pulled the same cotton throw blanket from the linen closet and settled in for some much-needed rest. Her eyes sagged, and her fingers throbbed. The injuries beneath the gauze needed to be cleaned and rewrapped; unfortunately, the first aid kit was in Aiden's bag.

With her thoughts on Aiden's bag, her mind snagged on the gun. Those hollow moments of desperation beneath the rock overhang had led Tess to believe that a bullet to the temple might be her only means of escape.

There had to be another way, right?

Tess's eyes fluttered shut. The moment one lid met the other, a shuffling sound in the bushes jolted them back open. She leaped from the recliner and pushed back a curtain, expecting to see Aiden approaching the cabin. All she saw was endless trees.

"Aiden?" she called out, loud enough for him to hear from outside. Tess was met with no response.

After pacing the floor and checking several more windows, she sat back down.

Exhaustion overtook her once more, and she lay on the brink of unconsciousness. A wild kaleidoscope of images bombarded her: Jacob screaming, her mother crying, Aiden bleeding out on the floor. Tess awoke in a cold sweat and was met with a scraping sound. It was reminiscent of the sound her chair made when she pushed it away from her work desk. It was coming from the office.

"Aiden?"

Creeping softly toward the office door, Tess's body was racked with fear. Her stomach felt hollow and her innards twisted as she pushed the door open. Aiden sat in the office chair, shuffling the deck of cards. When she entered, he looked up at her and smiled.

"Wake up, Tess."

Tess gasped awake and found herself still in the recliner. She pressed her palms into her closed eyes and groaned. Without warning, tears fell, wetting her hands and cheeks.

"I can't keep doing this!" Tess whimpered. Sleep was now something far from reach. She pulled her knees into her chest and wrapped her arms tightly around them. Though the position offered unfounded comfort, she would take what she could get.

Tess sat, steeling herself for the forest's next dose of malevolence, even creating new scenarios in her mind.

What will it be next?

Conjuring the most dreadful images in her mind, Tess saw Aiden dead and broken, her mother's walking corpse lecturing her through bloody lips, the forest wrapping its leafy tendrils around her and pulling in every direction until she was ripped into pieces.

It sounded peaceful, actually. Giving up. No longer awaiting a fresh terror at every turn. As Tess fell into a deep sleep, she contemplated simply surrendering to the woods and letting it do its worst until she withered away.

A banging sound yanked her from a restless slumber. Tess's eyes snapped open as something clattered against a door, or maybe the wood siding. Her surroundings were pitch black, and she determined the night was not yet over.

"Aiden?" Tess shouted. The only response was another aggressive bash of something against the house. Tess planted her feet on the floor, anticipating the moment that her eyes adjusted enough to see the nearer features within the cabin. There was only darkness.

The slamming intensified, closer now, and Tess bolted from the recliner. She managed a few steps until her toe snagged on the coffee table, and she plummeted toward the ground. As Tess fell, she threw her hands out to catch her fall. They slid against the oak table but were not enough to keep her from crashing into it headfirst. The corner met her head at the top of her hairline with force. Stars swirled in her eyes as she collapsed to the ground. Just before she lost consciousness, she realized why her eyes had never adjusted to the darkness of the room.

17

BUTTERFLY WINGS

As Tess came to, her forehead ached with a dull, steady pain. She touched a careful hand to the injury, wetting her fingers with a trickle of blood. As she felt around, Tess's fingers groped at dirt and leaves; she was lying on the forest floor.

Though her eyes were wide open, Tess saw nothing. At some point in the night, the forest had stolen her vision.

"Aiden?" Tess cried out. Though the effort was futile, she made it anyway as she needed someone now more than ever.

Tess pushed herself to a sitting position and tried to ignore the chill that had crept over her body. A thin layer of dew lingered on her skin, making her wonder how long she had been unconscious. Without any idea where she was,

Tess imagined herself amid a copse of trees, the cabin long gone.

The forest was quiet with anticipation, awaiting her next move. She felt like a lab rat being observed by a mad scientist. Anger boiled inside her as she felt the trees watching her. She could almost hear them.

"What if we destroy her hands? Let's separate her from her only friend. Ooh, take her sight. What will she do then?"

Whatever this place was, whatever happened here to blacken its soul, it embodied the most foul, depraved evil Tess could comprehend. The plagues of this land did not foster the sadistic tendencies of a serial killer, getting off on unique, twisted ways to end a life. Rather, it had the mentality of a troubled child who enjoyed pulling the wings off of butterflies just to watch them suffer.

A thought struck Tess, and she snickered.

I get it. Blinding Lights? Hilarious.

"Aiden!" Tess tried again. The smallest bit of hope that he might hear her kept her going. Though she could not see, if he were by her side to guide her through the woods, to navigate the horrors with her, to indulge in awful small talk, it would have made the situation substantially easier to cope with. Still, Aiden's voice did not make itself known.

Tess stood and listened. The forest's usual foreboding silence settled over her. She longed to hear running water, wind, or anything that suggested she still dwelled in an earthly place. The only sound was her own shallow breathing.

What's the plan, Tess? She curled and uncurled her fingers as her mind raced with what to do next. The urge to fall back to the ground and let the forest take her was overwhelming. Then, her mother's face appeared in her mind.

I'm going to find a way back to you, mom. I promise.

The dire aspects of the situation closed in on her—in the middle of the forest, no sense of direction, and no sounds to follow. Tess teetered on shaky legs and began walking. She held out her hands to catch any obstacles before smacking her face into them.

Tess's shoes pressed down on the ground with careful, measured steps. Each time a twig snapped beneath her feet, she flinched. The snapping sounds echoed behind her, conjuring images of something stalking her through the woods. Her eyes widened, as though she could lift her lids a certain degree and her sight would return. It did not.

Periodically, Tess called Aiden's name. There were no acoustics in the woods, nothing that deflected her shouts. They simply fell short as though absorbed by the leaves.

Rough, scratchy bark met her mangled fingertips, sending a jolt of pain through her arms. She felt around the tree and sidestepped it to continue on.

Leaves brushed against her, pricking at the laces melted into the tops of her feet. Swinging her hands out in front of her, Tess felt nothing. When she took a step, foliage brushed against her knees. She was walking into a bush.

Tess pulled her foot backward, and a stem caught her calf. She set her foot back down, attempted to lift it another way, and stumbled. Pain seared through her arms and her cheeks as she fell forward. Thorns lined every inch of the bush, and ripped at her skin with each movement. On all fours, Tess paused, trying to determine the best way out of the sharp branches.

Every direction Tess tried, thorns stabbed into her flesh, and tightened around her like a snare. She tugged her arms up and down, left and right. All motions lead to pain.

Tess started to crawl. Ignoring the barbs catching in her flesh and tearing it open, she pushed forward. Whimpers of agony escaped her lips as she ripped through the thorn bush. Pain enveloped her entire body, her knees digging into the dirt as she crept through, pulling shoots of the bush from the ground with her momentum.

A spike punctured the top of her eyelid, and she reared back, adjusting her head to move around it. Thorns snagged on her hair, ripping strands from her scalp. Tess's cheeks were sliced to shreds, and blood dribbled down her nose and chin.

After crawling and tearing through the bush for what seemed like hours, Tess's head pushed through an opening. Despite the stinging pain, Tess barrelled on until she was free. She fell to the ground, wailing and swiping thorns that had lodged into her skin. Dirt commingled with the open gashes, causing the misery to swell.

Tess steadied her breath and picked herself up from the forest floor. There was no time for groveling or maudlin episodes. She needed to keep moving.

After what felt like hours, Tess leaned against a tall, sturdy pine—at least that's what she pictured as her back rested against its coarse trunk. Her exhaustion made her feel as though she had traveled miles. She laughed to herself, imagining she had only moved a few feet since she started. Sliding down against the tree, Tess caught her breath and licked her parched lips.

Between Tess's fingers, a warm sticky liquid seeped through the gauze. The constant groping of her surroundings must have upset her wounds. Tears welled up in her eyes as she recalled the grotesque state of her hands. She swerved the emotions by telling herself that the injuries would be tended to the moment she found Aiden.

I'm so tired of lying to myself.

Tess huffed out a deep sigh and leaned her head back against the tree. With all the strength she could muster, Tess pushed away the sensations of hunger and thirst, the hopelessness of being lost in the woods, and the dread of never finding Aiden. Instead, she thought of her mother. The woman who had given up everything for Tess, loving her with every ounce of her being.

Tess wondered what day it was, how much time had passed. She figured it to be Sunday or Monday, yet the forest had proven to be a master of manipulation. For all she knew, it could be five minutes after she had parked the car. Or five weeks.

A terrible thought entered her mind. If enough time had passed, people would notice Tess's disappearance. Her mother would notice. If she came looking for her, her mother could wind up another victim of the forest.

Tess's eyes fluttered shut. She tried to fight it. She needed to keep moving. The days had been so difficult on her, though. Surely, she had earned a few moments of repose. Her head swam with fatigue, and Tess began to doze off.

"Tess, sweetheart."

The familiar voice pierced her ears and struck her in the heart.

"Mom?"

18

PLAN B

"I t's me, honey. What have you gotten yourself into out here?"

It's not real, it's not real, it's not real, Tess repeated, in hopes of resisting the urge to crawl desperately to her mother's voice.

"Tess?" The voice was identical to her mother's, warm and full of love. Tears sprang from Tess's eyes. She longed to curl into her mother's comforting embrace. The last time she would probably hear her mother's voice, and the instance was a farce.

A gentle hand gripped Tess's shoulder.

"Mom," Tess sobbed, and leaned her cheek against the fingers caressing her. The skin was cold, wet with a sticky liquid that clung to her cheek, and something gelatinous writhed against Tess's closed eye.

Get up, this isn't real. That's not my mother!

She sprang up from her resting spot. Her legs tangled together, causing her to stumble. Finding her balance, she pushed herself off the leafy forest floor and ran. A burning scream scorched Tess's throat as she fled.

"Aiden!" Tess cried out with desperation. She thought maybe if he heard the fear in her voice, he would come running, come to save her from whatever sinister entity stalked her. The only thing she heard in return was her feet pounding the dirt.

With hands splayed out in front, Tess dodged trees and scuffled through bushes. Thorns ripped at her calves and shins. Tears soaked her cheeks. The toe of her shoe jammed hard into a rock, flinging her through the air. As she met the ground, Tess slid against sharp twigs, and dirt filled her mouth. Leaves crunched behind her. Whatever had touched her shoulder was still after her.

Get up, get up, get up, Tess pleaded with herself.

Tess was running again, her heart hammering as icy fear took hold. Wind rushed past as her legs scurried away from the predator closing in on her.

The moment her foot hit it, Tess knew things were about to take a drastic turn. There was no ground beneath one shoe. And she had built up too much momentum to stop the other foot from extending outward.

Tess fell down a steep embankment. She reached out for anything to help slow the fall. A pointed rock yanked away the gauze holding her fingers intact. Spurts of blood pooled at the tips of her fingers. Her body slammed against the ground over and over, a helpless ragdoll jostled by nature, until she landed with a sickening thud.

The first breath she took was accompanied by labored rasps. The wind had been knocked from her lungs. Something was sliding down the hill toward her. She could just make out shoes shuffling through the leaves.

A viscous fluid slid down her forehead into her eyes. She touched a hand to her head to find it was partially caved in, bashed against a rock somewhere on the way down. The steady pulsing of her heartbeat pounded in her ears. Yet, that was not the worst of it.

A tingling sensation buzzed around her, just out of reach. She was aware of her torso, her arms, yet the lower half of her felt...gone. Her bloodied fingers moved in a frenzy around her to find she had landed against the thick trunk of a fallen tree.

Footsteps approached Tess, coming toward her with ominous speed. Placing her shredded hands on the ground, Tess tried to push herself away, but her legs would not move. A shiver ran through her as a wave of delirium threatened to overtake her consciousness.

"Please," she begged. The footsteps ended just beside her body. A soft hand touched her cheek. "Aiden?" The thumb of the hand rubbed back and forth against her skin. "Oh, Aiden!"

All Tess wanted was to hear his voice.

Aiden picked up one of Tess's hands in his, gently touching it to his throat. His Adam's apple bobbed beneath her hand, as though he were working at swallowing something. Then, he brought her hand to his lips. They felt tight, pursed.

"You can't speak," Tess realized, and felt Aiden's head nod in affirmation. Sobs erupted from Tess. She pulled Aiden into her and wrapped him in a fierce hug. Weeping transformed into laughter as she confronted the cruel trickery of the forest. Taking her sight, stomping out Aiden's voice—turning their survival into a demented game.

"Aiden, I hit my back really hard. My head, too. I think my fingers are getting infected. I think this is it. I tried really hard to keep going, to get the hell out of here. I think we need to do what we talked about before."

Tess squeezed her eyes shut and more tears spilled from her lids. Her body was broken. She had lost feeling in her legs. A feverish chill washed over her, and she was at the edge of consciousness. She listened as Aiden rifled through his pack. Then, he pulled her hand to his cheek, and she felt a wet stream of tears trailing down them. Aiden's erratic breathing entwined with her own ragged intakes to make a symphony of pain and failing flesh.

I'm sorry, mom.

The forest had won. Aiden had been right all along. The manipulations, the mind games, the disappearing acts, it all crescendoed until Tess was left wanting to die. Even at the cost of never seeing her mother again. Just like Aiden's sister, Tess's body would likely never be found, leaving her mother to fret and search until she lost hope.

Tess flinched when the cold gun barrel pressed against her temple. Aiden's hand shook, hesitation stealing away the seconds. Tess steeled herself, looking forward to the end of her agony, the end of the forest's games. She closed her eyes and nodded. Aiden pulled the trigger.

EPILOGUE

Tess lay on the forest floor, blood pooling beneath her head. Her body nothing more than a doll, ripped apart and broken at the seams. The gun still sat in Aiden's trembling hand. A thin wisp of smoke wafted from the barrel and evaporated into the air.

Once he pulled the trigger, the bullet blasted through Tess's skull, boring into her brain. She was lifeless within seconds. Pieces of bone and spatters of blood sprayed the surrounding area, painting it with the last of what she had to offer to the woods.

Aiden held the pistol up to his own temple. Each time, it was a new game. Just when he thought he had figured out some rule or found some loophole, the forest morphed into something even more evil than before. He eased his finger on the trigger, then let out a tight, bitter laugh and tossed the gun to the ground. He had already played this game, and look where it had gotten him.

Tess looked beautiful lying there, despite the sunken-in part of her scalp. Even through the sheen of sweat, the dirt crusted around her mouth, the blood weeping from every part of her. Tess was no different than the many others he had encountered in these woods: a kind soul trying to escape an unkind world.

Aiden had hoped he could save this one, though. He really tried.

So stupid, so naive, Aiden cursed himself. *Next time will be different.*

Next time. Maybe it was the card game. They had gotten too friendly. The forest did not like that.

Aiden shoved the gun back into his bag and zipped it up. He stood, casting one last wistful glance at the fractured woman, then turned to disappear into the woods.

Next time will be different.

PLAYLIST

I Let It in and It Took Everything—**Loathe, Vincent Void**

Into the Earth—**Lorna Shore**

All I Do is Sink—**the Amity Affliction**

Blinding Lights—**the Weeknd**

Salt—**The Devil Wears Prada**

All of This Is Fleeting—**Polaris**

Let Me Leave—**Currents**

Paralyzed—**Memphis May Fire**

Bones—**Make Them Suffer**

Pet—**A Perfect Circle**

Bad Dream—**Ruelle**

Collapse—**After the Burial**

Phantom Pain—**Saving Vice**

Acknowledgements

To Jesus, my strength when I have none, my peace when I unravel.

To my mom, always my biggest fan.

To my family and friends, thank you for supporting me and always cheering me on.

To my editor Bill, for helping me to finetune this story, for always being there for questions and advice, and helping me battle the dreaded imposter syndrome.

To the Dark Veil Society, thank you for answering all of my questions no matter how simple, always being supportive, and providing great memes.

To J.L. Engel, for helping me name this eerie tale.

To the entire writing community for being so supportive, you all are the friends I didn't know I needed and can't live without. Thanks for following my journey, and I'm honored to be following yours.

THE DARK VEIL SOCIETY

To find your next indie horror read, visit
www.darkveilsociety.com

Coming Soon

The Prologue of Without A Whisper: Song 2 of the Tangled Elegies

Kate lay curled in the fetal position, sweating and shivering against the floor tiles. Vomit filled the toilet beside her, chunks of regurgitated canned goods spattered across the porcelain and ceramic.

Kate pushed herself into a sitting position and took deep, gulping breaths. An acrid taste coated her tongue. A fire trailed down her esophagus, igniting pain each time she swallowed. A yawn forced her mouth open, and her eyes threatened to close as their lids drooped with exhaustion.

Freedom was finally within her grasp. Kate never dared believed she would escape Connor and his depraved torments. The end result would inevitably be Connor tiring of her and dispatching her in a way she dared not imagine. The human body could only endure so many beatings and neglect, and hers was sure to succumb to malnutrition or infection.

There were times, however, when Kate allowed herself to dream. She dared imagine someone coming to her aid and rescuing her. She never expected a disease to eradicate society, creeping into humans until they lost control of their limbs and their minds and developing an appetite for flesh. Covered in her own filth, groveling on the floor beside the commode was not how she pictured herself after these delirious liberations. If this was the price for freedom, she would gladly pay with all that she had.

Navigating the upturned world had been precarious, at best. Kate had found herself stumbling from one home to the next, in urgent need of food and barely able to fend off the Infected she met along the way. Once a home started to feel secure, the provisions thinned, forcing her to move on. Which eventually led her to this home, chosen in haste after her limbs burned with anguish and the nausea gripped her insides.

Kate exited the bathroom and scanned the closed doors in the hallway. She chose the one closest, craving only a soft, warm bed to collapse into. Extending her arm to the doorknob was enough to send aches pulsing along her bones. The determination to rest overpowered the pain.

When Kate pushed the door open, she strode toward the bed, only to freeze in place. An Infected stood on the far side of the bed, gaping at her. Drool spilled over its cracked lips along with a low, rumbling groan. The creature only needed a moment's gaze at Kate's tender flesh before it lunged. Its bruised, knobby legs propelled themselves clumsily after her.

Kate dashed from the room and pulled the door closed, if only to buy some time, and took off toward the stairs. The Infected barreled through the doorway behind her, and heavy footfalls grew closer. Kate's feet plodded down the first few steps until her throbbing muscles gave way. Her knees buckled and ankles bent until she was plummeting down the steps, head and limbs thumping against the hardwood with each impact.

Once the fall had ended, Kate lay face down at the bottom of the stairs. The Infected descended two steps at a time, eyes fixated on its next meal. Kate cried out as she lifted her battered body from the floor. A wave of nausea nearly doubled her over, and she fought the urge to expel what contents of her stomach remained.

Forcing her feet to move, Kate shambled through the house. When her right leg weakened, she grabbed onto a side table in the hall, grasping for stability. Picture frames and a flower vase crashed to the floor as her shaking hands groped along the wooden surface.

When she entered the kitchen, Kate knew she was not up for a chase. The time to make her stand was now. She searched the counters and spotted a suitable weapon. The monster rounded the corner just as Kate lifted a cast iron skillet from the kitchen island. The Infected stared at her, watching her movements curiously as though understanding her intentions. The Infected's face turned from side to side, then it released a gravelly snarl.

When the creature stepped closer, Kate lifted the cast iron pan like a baseball bat, despite her feeble muscles. Her body quaked as adrenaline merged with fear, but she had not come this far just to be eaten alive days after her escape.

Kate drew in her breath, then let out a ferocious scream. The Infected recoiled a few inches, its black eyes seemingly curious to the sound. Kate drew the skillet back and swung it with all of her strength. The iron pummeled the Infected's mouth with an explosion of cracking bone. The lower half of the creature's jaw swung loosely from its skull, connected only on one side. The collision sent the diseased monster stumbling sidelong until it crashed against the fridge.

The overexerted muscles in Kate's arms pleaded with her to rest. Instead, she slammed the pan against the creature again, shattering the bones around its temple. Its hair reddened with gore as blood seeped to the surface. The Infected made a desperate, furious sound, and its arms thrashed toward Kate, nearly grabbing her vomit-soaked shirtsleeve.

Kate stepped backward on weary legs. Her lungs heaved with effort. Every body part ached and cried out in anguish, longing for respite. Nevertheless, Kate lifted the hefty skillet with the last ounce of strength she had and swung. The Infected's head caved in, and it slumped to the floor.

Standing over the Infected, Kate gazed at the fleshy mosaic of bones and blood and tissue. Once she was certain the creature was dead, Kate staggered and fell to the floor. Goosebumps crawled across her skin as chilled sweat formed a film over her body. She gazed up at the ceiling, tears stinging the corners of her eyes. Nausea clamped its vice grip around her abdomen, and she sat up just before vomiting on the floor.

After several moments of dry heaving, the muscles in her stomach relaxed. Kate steadied her shuddering breaths, then impelled her wobbly legs to carry her back upstairs. She did a quick scan of the remaining bedrooms before finding a suitable bed to topple into with an exhale of relief.

For hours, Kate tossed and turned on the mattress, perspiring and shivering, ignoring bouts of stomach cramps, and dipping in and out of fever dreams. Even when her body seemed relaxed, her mind raged—flooded with memories, fears, and incoherent thoughts.

Instead of the sleep Kate desperately needed, she lay there in quiet suffering as the opioid Connor kept coursing through her body worked its way out. Kate being held hostage and subjected to a man's sadistic cravings had not been enough. Fighting and killing for her freedom had not been enough. Now, Kate would battle through days of grueling withdrawal from a drug she never wanted in her system to begin with. Connor was sure to be laughing at her from beyond the grave for thinking her woes ended with his death.

Though the pain was immense and the world uncertain, this felt like the final step. Once the poison had run its course, all traces of Connor would be eviscerated. And it made Kate feel bulletproof.

Printed in Dunstable, United Kingdom